DAVID COPPERFIELD

Charles Dickens

retold by Jenny Dooley

Express Publishing

Published by Express Publishing
Liberty House, New Greenham Park,
Newbury, Berkshire RG19 6HW
Tel: (0044) 1635 817 363 – Fax: (0044) 1635 817 463
e-mail: inquiries@expresspublishing.co.uk
http://www.expresspublishing.co.uk

© Jenny Dooley, 2003

Design & Illustration © Express Publishing, 2003

First published 2003

ISBN   1-84466-375-2

Colour Illustrations: Nathan & Stone

Contents

Introductory Lesson

Charles Dickens

Charles Dickens was born near Portsmouth, England, on February 7th, 1812. He was the second of eight children, whose father, John, was a clerk for the Navy. Although Charles had an idyllic early family life, his father was a poor manager of money

Before Reading

1. In pairs, answer the following questions:
   a Look at the front cover of the book. What can you see in the picture?
   b When do you think the story takes place?
   · c Read the blurb on the back cover and discuss what kind of difficulties you think David Copperfield might have experienced.

2. Look at the following pictures. How do you think they are connected to the story?

1
2
3
4

5
6
7

and got into financial difficulties. Eventually, he was put in prison, where his family later joined him. It was common in those days for the family of a debtor to live with him in prison. Charles was taken out of school and went to work putting labels on bottles of shoe polish. He worked long hours for very little money and lived away from his family, alone in London. He became a clerk in a lawyer's office when he was 15 and also worked as a reporter in the evenings. At 18, he fell in love with a pretty and careless girl, but the affair ended unhappily for Dickens after three years.

These events from his early life affected him deeply and he used these experiences to write his novels. Dickens wrote about 'David Copperfield', his eighth novel, "Of all my books I like this the best". It is largely autobiographical and was published in monthly parts between May 1849 and November 1850. Dickens wrote a total of fourteen complete novels and died in 1870 before completing 'The Mystery of Edwin Drood'. He is buried in Westminster Abbey in London.

3. Read the information about Charles Dickens and answer the questions that follow.

a   When was Charles Dickens born?

b   How many brothers and sisters did Charles Dickens have?

c   What was Dickens' first job?

d   How old was Dickens when he started to work for the lawyer?

e   When was 'David Copperfield' published?

f   What was the name of Dickens' unfinished novel?

g   When did Dickens die?

Young David

Mr Murdstone

Clara Copperfield

Peggotty

Uriah Heep

David and Agnes

Mr Micawber

Mr Peggotty and Emily

Aunt Betsey

Beginnings

I was born in Blunderstone, Suffolk. We lived in a nice house with a garden and many trees outside. My father had named our house 'The Rookery' because a type of bird – the rook – had nests in the trees all around our property.

It was after my father's death, and just before my birth, that his aunt, Betsey Trotwood, came to our home. Things were about to change at The Rookery, and my life was about to begin. Aunt Betsey marched into our house and gave everybody her opinions from the beginning!

"My nephew, David, was a good man. But like all men, he was a bit silly."

My mother was usually shy, but on this occasion, she told Aunt Betsey firmly that she did not like her to speak in an unkind way about my deceased father.

"Please, Madam! I will not have you talk about my late husband in this manner! My husband, David Copperfield, was a good and honest man with a heart of gold. If this baby is a son, I shall call him David Copperfield like him, and I hope that he will be exactly like his father!"

Aunt Betsey folded her arms and stared at my mother.

"The baby will be a girl! I will be her godmother and her name shall be Betsey. And she certainly will **not** make the mistakes in life that **I** did!"

Of course, Aunt Betsey was very disappointed when I was born. Her attitude towards males was a bit harsh. This was because of the problems she had had with her husband when she was married. He had treated her badly, and they were eventually

separated. Therefore, she seemed to feel that all men were wicked or silly, and that they made women's lives difficult.

When she first came, she knew that my mother was a young widow expecting a baby, and with only one servant, Peggotty. Aunt Betsey had declared that she had come to The Rookery to help my mother look after me.

Unfortunately, the fact that I was born a male was too much of a shock for Aunt Betsey. She couldn't bear it and left the house in a huff immediately after my birth. And so, we were left all alone, just the three of us. Luckily, dear Peggotty was much more than a servant. She was a good friend to my mother, and me as well.

Although it did not seem at all like a good beginning for me, we made the most of our life together and were happy. In the evenings or on cold wet days, my young and beautiful mother would sit with Peggotty in the parlour. They would chat by the fire and would often sing or read to me. Then they would rock me in their arms. When I fell asleep, they would take me to my bed and kiss me warmly on my forehead. On Sundays, we would walk to the nearby church, and visit my father's grave. Knowing that he was close by made me feel safe.

Even though I was very young at the time, I have many tender memories of my early life. Those sweet moments will remain in my heart forever. I think back and sometimes laugh to myself when I remember particular moments from that peaceful and pleasant time. I used to think that Peggotty's plump, red cheeks looked so much like apples that every time she went outdoors, I would tell her to take care. I was sure the birds would think that her cheeks were juicy apples and peck at them!

How things changed when Mr Murdstone entered our lives! I was about five years old the first time we met. He looked down at me and said,

"Give me your hand, boy! A man must have a firm handshake if he wants to get anywhere in the world."

He began walking my mother home from the church. Then he would visit her at home, and stay a little longer each time. He was a handsome man – tall and slim with dark hair and a beard. Mother would dress up and curl her hair before Mr Murdstone came to see her. She would giggle when he was at the house and sometimes her face would become red. I do admit, I **was** jealous, but this wasn't the reason why I didn't like him.

I didn't trust him because of the look he had in his eyes. They were small and dark, and didn't seem kind at all. Later, I was proved to be correct.

Mr Murdstone wanted to be alone with Mother, so Peggotty was told to take me away for a few weeks to visit her brother in Yarmouth.

"What a treat it'll be, Master Davy! There's the sea, the boats and the fishermen! And young ones to play with!"

I was excited because I was going somewhere new, but I would miss Mother very much.

My First Trip and Homecoming

When I first arrived in Yarmouth I was disappointed. I don't know what I expected, but I certainly did not think that the seaside would be so dull and gloomy. However, I soon cheered up when I met Peggotty's relatives – her friendly and jolly brother, Mr Peggotty, his nephew, Ham, and his niece, Emily, who was also an orphan. Emily was the same age as me and when I saw her, it was love at first sight!

Mr Peggotty's widowed sister-in-law, Mrs Gummidge, lived there too. She seemed miserable, and complained all the time. I don't think she realised how lucky she was to be with such good people.

They all lived in a strange but wonderful place: a large boat that had been turned into a house. It no longer sailed on the water, but was now permanently on the beach. It was divided into little rooms with proper furniture, and pictures on the walls. There was even a fireplace! Every room was painted in bright colours. The place had a fishy smell, of course, but it wasn't at all unpleasant!

While I was at Yarmouth, I spent most of my days collecting stones and shells on the beach with Emily. One day a dreamy, distant look came into Emily's eyes and she told me her secret wish.

"If I was a lady, I'd buy Uncle Peggotty a gold watch and a silver pipe! Oh, and a red velvet waistcoat with diamond buttons on it because he's been so good to me – and my third cousin, Ham."

Then her smile disappeared.

"I don't think I'll ever become a lady, though … My father was only a fisherman and my mother was a fisherman's daughter, so I don't suppose I'm from the right sort of family …"

Her beautiful eyes looked so sad that I wished I could do something to help make her wish come true.

My holiday came to an end too soon and we had to part. I was very sad to leave 'little' Emily, but we promised to write to each other. She was my first love and I would never forget her.

When I arrived back home, I found that everything had changed. Mother had married Mr Murdstone, and his sister had come to live there. It just didn't feel like home anymore. Even my mother seemed to be different. She rarely spoke to me, and when she did it was in a quick whisper.

"Davy, I love you. But please, please behave."

I felt lonely, and cried every night for hours before I fell asleep. Mr Murdstone had not only changed the atmosphere of The Rookery, but he had also changed Mother. She feared him and his sister. If Mother showed me any kindness, he would frown at her, then take her aside and talk to her in a strict way. I felt so sorry for Mother.

"Remember that I am teaching you how to be a good mother. Be firm with the boy and always control yourself. Your son needs discipline!"

Mother would lower her head, and I sometimes saw tears in her eyes.

One day, I went into the living room after breakfast for my morning lessons with Mother. Mr and Miss Murdstone sat and listened carefully to everything she said, and watched everything she did.

She smiled at me when she thought the Murdstones weren't looking. But Mr Murdstone saw her and decided to ask me a question.

"How much will I have to pay for 5000 pieces of cheese if each one costs four and a half pennies?"

I was so afraid that I couldn't answer the question. I saw Miss Murdstone smile at her brother.

"He doesn't know the answer, Edward."

Mr Murdstone stood up then and I saw that he held a cane in his hand. He swished the cane and I heard it whistle through the air.

"When I was a boy and didn't know my lessons, I was beaten. It did me no harm – and it will do you no harm either, David."

My mother begged Mr Murdstone to give me another chance. But he refused to listen.

"David and I will go upstairs and I'll teach him a lesson he'll never forget!"

Mr Murdstone dragged me up to my room and held my head under his arm so that I could not move, then he beat me with the cane until I thought I would die. I begged him to stop, but he just beat me harder, so I did the only thing I could. I bit his hand. This made Mr Murdstone very angry. He beat me again, then when I couldn't stand up any more, he threw me to the floor, left the room and locked the door behind him.

"That will teach you a lesson, Copperfield, and you'll have plenty of time to think about your behaviour!"

I was left there alone for five days. Mother and Peggotty were not allowed to come near me. Only dear Peggotty whispered to me one night through the keyhole.

"Mr Murdstone has decided to send you away to boarding school. I'll never forget you, Master Davy. I love you and so does your mother!"

Those words meant so much to me, and I would remember them whenever I was alone.

19

School Days

On the morning I left for school, my mother said goodbye quickly, and then I was on my way to London. When I first saw the city, I thought it was an amazing place. There were tall chimneys and a large bridge that I later found out was called London Bridge. But, I was very disappointed when I saw my school.

Salem House was in an old building that looked like it was ready to fall down. The boys there were loud and noisy but they were friendly, except when the Headmaster, Mr Creakle, was present. He walked up and down and stared at us with a look of disgust on his face. He shouted at us and then chose a few of us to beat with his cane. We were all very scared of Mr Creakle.

The only pupil who Mr Creakle did not beat was Steerforth. I considered him to be the bravest and most handsome boy at the school. Steerforth and I became friends. He liked me because I would tell stories at night from books that I used to read at home.

I also had many unpleasant memories of Salem house. On cold, frosty mornings when the bell rang, we dragged ourselves out of bed into the dark and damp classrooms. We ate meals of boiled beef and stale bread before we returned to the classrooms, where we worked until it was time to go to bed.

At last holiday time came and I returned home for a break. I walked into the parlour where I had spent many happy days when I was very young. I was surprised when I saw my mother holding a baby! Mother seemed pale and weak. I ran to her. When I hugged my dear mother, the baby in her arms put its tiny fingers to my lips.

"Davy, my dear child, this is your brother!"

From the very first moment I loved my little half-brother. I spent as much time as I could, holding him and patting him gently –

except when Mr Murdstone's sister, Miss Murdstone, was about. Her dislike of me was very obvious. Once, when she saw me holding my baby brother, she told me never to touch him again. My mother and I were shocked, but of course Mother said nothing. She seemed even more afraid of the Murdstones than ever.

On another occasion during those same school holidays, my mother compared the baby's eyes to mine. She said proudly that they were similar in shape and colour. Miss Murdstone told her never to compare her brother's baby to me and said that the baby and I were not alike in any way.

Mr Murdstone, too, was cruel to me and said that I was evil and lazy. I was almost looking forward to going back to school, where I wasn't always made to feel unwelcome and where at least I had friends and enjoyed my schoolwork.

I returned to Salem House and everything seemed to be satisfactory. At the time, I thought the most terrible thing was to be hit by Mr Creakle's cane.

But soon, something happened that was much worse, and it affected my life in the most terrible way. One day, Mr Creakle called me into his office and gave me the most dreadful news.

"Copperfield, your mother is dead and you're to go home immediately. Pack your bags!"

When I arrived home, Peggotty told me that Mother had become weaker and more ill after I had left. A day after my mother died, my little brother passed away as well. I was very sad, shocked and lonely. I was only ten, and all alone in the world. I was an orphan.

I went to the funeral and Mother was buried in the same churchyard near my home where my Father was buried. That day, even the light outdoors seemed sad and more gloomy than usual.

CLARA
MURDSTONE
1812-1839

EDWARD
MURDSTONE
1839

DAVID
COPPERFIELD
1807-1839

Off to Work I Go

*E*verything had changed. Peggotty no longer lived at The Rookery, because the Murdstones told her to leave. She had met a cart driver named Barkis and they got married and moved to Yarmouth. Before she left The Rookery, she tried to comfort me about the death of my mother and baby brother. She told me that she still loved me and suggested that I visit Yarmouth again for a while. The Murdstones agreed immediately, because they wanted my home to themselves.

Yarmouth did not seem as exciting to me as it had been when I first met Peggotty's family. Little Emily was as beautiful as ever, but she acted like a grown-up and didn't talk to me as much. However, I still loved her and when I told her that I would protect her forever, she laughed at me.

"Oh, David! You're so childish!"

Unfortunately the time came when I had to go back to The Rookery – and the Murdstones. They made sure that I no longer felt at home. From the moment I arrived, and for months afterwards, they ignored me. I was so lonely and bored, but the worst thing was that the Murdstones decided not to send me back to school. I was very sad about this.

"People like you do not need an education. Anyway, it is far too expensive. You will have to learn to make your own way in the world – and the sooner you start, the better!"

So Mr Murdstone sent me to London to work in his wine factory, 'Murdstone and Grinby's'. Even though I was only eleven years old, I worked for over ten hours a day for a very low wage. The factory was in a dark, damp and smelly warehouse, which was full of rats. The other workers were rough and used bad language. I wasn't like these people and I missed Steerforth and the other boys – my friends from Salem House.

Luckily, Mr Murdstone had arranged for me to stay with a family called the Micawbers while I was in London. Even though they did not have much, they were friendly people. I was glad to be a part of their family, because I had been lonely and miserable for too long. Many people came knocking on their door asking for money that Mr Micawber owed them. Mr Micawber was a kind-hearted man, but he was rather irresponsible.

In the end, he had to go to prison, because he did not have enough money to pay his debts. I went and visited him often. On one of my visits, Mr Micawber gave me advice based on his own hard life.

"Annual income, twenty pounds; annual expenses, nineteen pounds; result – happiness! Annual income, twenty pounds; annual expenses, twenty-one pounds; result – misery! Remember that, Copperfield!"

Mr Micawber then began to sob.

"It's wise to save, David. I never had a job to pay me twenty pounds. Oh, I've looked for a job but I'll only work for good people. And the odd jobs I've had here and there have paid such poor wages that I couldn't possibly save. Why, I have a family to feed! So I had to borrow and now I can't pay my debts … and I'm stuck here in misery!"

I tried to cheer Mr Micawber up by telling him that I would most certainly take his advice and try to save money.

"I promise you, Sir, that I will remember your words, and will always try to put aside some money 'for a rainy day', as the saying goes."

27

With that he cheered up and began a jolly song that I do believe he made up.

"Always save for a rainy day, a rainy day, a rainy day,
Always save for a rainy day,
Because the sun won't always shine your way … !"

When Mr Micawber's prison sentence was over, he decided that he and his family would leave London. I could not bear to stay in London alone. Nor could I bear to continue working in that dirty factory, sticking labels on bottles, surrounded by people swearing and fighting.

I decided to run away. The only person I could think of to turn to was Aunt Betsey Trotwood – the relative who had visited us at The Rookery on the day I was born.

With My Aunt

I had overheard conversations between my mother and Peggotty, so I knew that my aunt lived in Dover – seventy miles from London. I decided to leave for Dover by coach.

My box, with my clothes and few possessions in it, was too heavy for me to carry all the way to the coach station, and a young man with a donkey and cart offered to take it to the coach station for a small fee. I agreed. But before I knew it, he had snatched both my money and my box, and drove off quickly in his rattling old cart, never to be seen again. The only way I could reach Dover now was by walking, because everything I had, including my money, had been stolen.

So I began my journey to Aunt Betsey's on foot. I walked until my shoes fell apart and my feet bled. I slept in fields, or under trees, like the beggars and tramps that I met on the way. I was very hungry and sold some of the clothes that I was wearing to buy food. So now the last things my mother had given me were gone.

At last I arrived in Dover. I found out where Betsey Trotwood lived by asking people in the town. She had a neat little cottage with a garden full of sweet-smelling flowers. I felt embarrassed standing in front of such a cheerful and well-kept house because I looked like a tramp – dirty and tired.

I took a deep breath when I saw a tall woman with a straight back walk out of the house. This was Aunt Betsey for sure! She looked very bossy and gardening tools were sticking out of her pockets. She was wearing a pair of large gardening gloves and she had a knife in her hand! I was about to turn and run away, but I reminded myself of my purpose, and approached her. She was shocked to see such a dirty boy at her door.

"Go away! Go along! No boys here!"

I watched her with my heart in my mouth as she marched back into her garden. But I was too desperate to leave now. I went in quietly and stood beside her. Then I put my hand on her arm.

"If you please, Ma'am …"

She turned and looked at me.

"If you please … Aunt."

"Eh?" she said, amazed.

"If you please, Aunt, I am your nephew."

"Oh, my!" said my aunt and sat down on the garden path.

"I am David Copperfield, of Blunderstone, in Suffolk – where you came on the night I was born and saw my dear Mama. I have been very unhappy since she died. I have been thrown out of my home, and removed from my school. I've been put to work that was not fit for me. It made me run away to you. I was robbed when I set out on my journey to find you and so walked all the way, and I have not slept in a bed since I began the journey."

I showed her my torn clothes and at this point all my strength left me. I burst into tears and could not stop. My aunt looked at me with a shocked expression and then took me by the hand and led me quickly into her parlour. She first gave me food to eat and then put me on the sofa, with a shawl under my head and her own handkerchief under my feet. She sat on the floor beside me and looked at me, unable to do anything but stare.

After some time, and when I had stopped crying, she asked Mr Dick to show me where the bathroom was so that I could have a bath. He was a kind old man who rented a room in my aunt's house. Later, I told my aunt all the details of my short but incredible life. Her eyes became wider and she looked down at the floor.

31

"You have been through quite a lot for a twelve-year-old boy!"

"That's why I had to come here. You're the only person I could think of who might help me."

"Oh, this is a difficult situation! I must think! I must think!"

Aunt Betsey walked up and down whenever she thought over a problem. Finally, she asked Mr Dick for his advice.

"What do you think, Mr Dick? What would you do with the boy?"

"I – I would put him to bed."

For the first time in months I slept in a soft and comfortable bed. I was so tired that I slept through all of the next day and night! When I woke up, I smelled fresh-baked bread from the kitchen, and heard birds singing outside the window. But, to my horror, when I went downstairs I saw Mr Murdstone and his sister in the parlour – talking with my aunt and Mr Dick. Mr Dick looked worried, and my aunt's back seemed even stiffer than usual. She looked very serious.

"Oh … I know very well how David's poor young mother suffered because of you and your sister! You are tyrants! And I know how badly you treated that poor boy! Leave my house at once, and never come back!"

The Murdstones were horrified.

"You will find out for yourself what an evil boy he is, Miss Trotwood!" said Mr Murdstone as they left the house.

"And keep off my lawn!" shouted Aunt Betsey as she slammed the door behind them.

I wanted to clap my hands in delight! My aunt was so brave! When they had gone, my aunt smiled at me.

"I don't believe a word they said, David. From now on, we'll do what's best for you. All I ask is that you respect us and follow our simple rules."

Life with the Wickfields

Sometimes my aunt was strict. She chased away the donkeys, or anyone else for that matter, who dared to walk over the grass near her garden. But she cared about me. Living there was like something from a storybook.

And I liked Mr Dick. He was an interesting person. His family thought he was mad and wanted to place him in a psychiatric institution, but Aunt Betsey let him stay with her. I must admit that Mr Dick was a bit odd at times, but he was gentle and kind. He was writing a book about his life. Aunt Betsey told me that he had been writing it for years, but he never seemed to finish it.

The time soon came when I had to go to school again. My aunt took the advice of her trusted friend and lawyer, Mr Wickfield, and I was enrolled at a school in Canterbury. Dr Strong was the headmaster there, and he was a polite and well-educated man. Aunt Betsey had arranged for me to live with Mr Wickfield while I was away at school.

I enjoyed living with Mr Wickfield and his lovely daughter, Agnes, who was thirteen – the same age as me. She had long brown hair and clear blue eyes. Agnes seemed very mature for her age and I often thought about what a wise and special person she was. She was like a sister. I trusted her and asked for her advice about many things.

"Agnes, I often think of my future and I don't know what I will do."

"Of course you don't. No one knows the future. But you can prepare for it by doing well at school and learning from your mistakes."

The only bad thing about living at the Wickfields was Uriah Heep, Mr Wickfield's assistant. Uriah Heep was a skinny young man

with greasy hair and long, ink-stained fingers, but it was more his manner that bothered me than his appearance. When he spoke he twisted his body in a strange way, which reminded me of a snake. From the first moment I saw him, my instincts told me not to trust him. He pretended to be humble and lowered his head a lot when he talked to us, but I often caught him grinning slyly when he said,

"I'm well aware that I am the humblest person in the world. My mother is likewise a very humble person. We live in a very humble house."

I was a bit uneasy one day when he insisted that I have tea with him and his mother. She was just as mysterious and frightening as her son. While we were having tea, they both asked me many strange questions.

"Do you know how much money Wickfield makes in a year?"

"Where's your family from, Master Copperfield? They must have money to send you to Dr Strong's school."

I answered truthfully, but I was very uncomfortable, and wondered why they asked such questions. Then, just as I was about to leave, there was a knock at the door. I was very surprised when I saw who it was – Mr Micawber, my old friend from London!

"Ah, David, my boy, you'll find that I turn up in many places where you don't expect me."

When I saw Mr Micawber and Uriah Heep being so friendly with each other, I felt a bit shocked, but I was happy to see my old friend again.

Time passed peacefully, and I eventually finished school when I was eighteen. I did very well in all my subjects. In fact, I got top marks! The time had also come for me to leave Canterbury and to start my own life. However, it was difficult for me to say goodbye to Agnes. We were both very sad, but something more serious seemed to be troubling her.

"David, I'm so worried about my father. Uriah Heep is an evil man. I don't trust him. He encourages Father to drink a lot of wine and then tells him not to worry and that **he** will look after the business. Promise me, David, that you will come and help us if we ever need it."

"Of course, Agnes. Of course I will!"

Old and New Friends

I finally chose a profession. After discussions with my aunt, I
decided to become a lawyer. My training began at the very old
but grand-looking law offices of 'Spenlow and Jorkins' in London.
My aunt was very helpful and found me a small but cosy room
to rent nearby.

Oh, how confident and free I felt living in London as a young
bachelor! I went out most evenings as I now had money to enjoy
myself. One night, when I was leaving the theatre, I saw my old
school friend, Steerforth. He still had thick blond hair and was
more handsome than ever. We shook hands warmly and Steerforth
told me that he was now a student at Oxford University.

"I always knew you'd be a success, Steerforth! You look just like
you did back at Salem House, only better – and older, of course!"

"I must say you're looking very well too, Daisy. You still look
young and innocent … and fresh!"

Steerforth had always liked to call me 'Daisy', ever since our days
at Salem House. When he first saw me, he had said that I reminded
him of 'a fresh daisy at sunrise'. And I quite liked the nickname myself.

Steerforth and I saw each other quite often while he was in
London and we became close again. I even asked him to come
and visit the Peggottys in Yarmouth with me. I wasn't sure what
he'd think of their simple ways, because he was from a different
social class. But, from the moment we arrived in Yarmouth, Steerforth
seemed to love everything about it.

"It's incredible that they made a home out of this old boat!"

On many occasions we sat inside Mr Peggotty's house, drinking,
eating and laughing with the Peggottys. We had arrived at a good
time, because the family were celebrating Ham and Emily's

38

engagement. I was happy for Emily but I would always remember her as 'little' Emily. Ham was a good-hearted and hard-working fellow and Emily, a young woman now, worked as a dressmaker. She seemed satisfied with her life, but I think that our stories about London reminded her of the old desire she had to be a 'lady'. When Steerforth spoke, that desire seemed to come back.

"London sounds so exciting! I wish I could live there."

"Then, why don't you? And I could show you around."

"Steerforth! Emily and Ham are going to be married, and they will live here."

"Oh, yes. I forgot! Well then, a toast to life and happiness by the sea!"

We all raised our glasses, but Emily did not look very happy.

Steerforth seemed to like the fisherman's life in Yarmouth. He even bought a boat before we left. He called it the *Little Emily*. I thought this was strange, but it didn't mean much to me at the time.

We went back to London and I was very busy with my training at 'Spenlow and Jorkins'. I was doing well at the office, so Mr Spenlow invited me to his house for dinner one evening. It was then that I met his beautiful and delicate daughter, Dora. I immediately fell madly in love with her and don't know how I concentrated on my work after that. I'd spend hours daydreaming about Dora – my princess.

I chased Dora for months, until she finally agreed to marry me. Everything in my life seemed to be going well. I worked part-time as a writer and saved enough money to buy us a little house. Everyone was happy for me, particularly Aunt Betsey. She would often hug me and say, "I was a fool for leaving you and your mother when you were born. You've turned out better than any niece I could have hoped for!"

Agnes seemed happy for me too, and she and Dora became best friends – even though they were so very different from each other. Although they were the same age, Agnes seemed older and wiser, and my Dora acted like a sweet child, sometimes sighing and playing with the curls in her hair.

"Davy, I'm a silly little thing. Perhaps you should have chosen someone clever like Agnes instead of me."

"What are you saying, my love? Hush now. I love you as you are, more than anything in the world!"

"In the world! Oh, David, the world's a large place!"

An Unsettling Time

One day I came home to find Mr Peggotty sitting in my parlour, with his head in his hands. He looked so sad that I expected the worst. At first I didn't understand what was wrong.

"I'll look all over the world until I find my Emily! I've raised her since she was a little girl. She's a good girl. She may have made mistakes ... but I'll always forgive her and I'll always be here to help her and protect her!"

After listening to him for some time I discovered that Emily and Steerforth had run away together! How could Steerforth have done something like that to the Peggottys? And what about Ham, who was so in love with Emily? He would have done anything for her. But Emily always wanted to be a 'lady' and she probably thought that Steerforth would make her one. Poor Mr Peggotty! Poor Ham! Poor Emily!

I decided to see Ham in Yarmouth and was about to leave when a letter arrived. It was from Agnes. She was in London, and wanted to see me urgently. She said it was very important. I rushed to see her, and realised that she was very upset.

"Oh, David, you must help us! My father and Uriah Heep are going to become business partners. Uriah Heep is still encouraging my father to drink too much. I think he's tricking Father by pretending to be a good and honest man, but I believe he's stealing money from the business!"

I held Agnes' hands in mine.

"Don't worry, Agnes. I'll do everything I can to help you and your father."

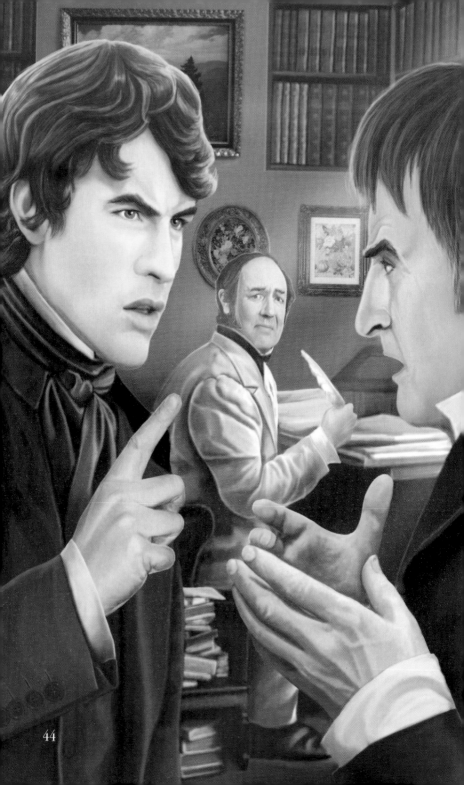

I went to see Heep at once, at Mr Wickfield's house, and I was shocked to find Mr Micawber working at Heep's desk.

"Mr Micawber, how can you work for a man like Heep?"

"Mr Heep is my employer now and I must respect the man who helps me pay my debts, David. Work is work."

I found Mr Micawber's behaviour to be rather peculiar. He had always said that he would only work for honest people. And somehow, Micawber seemed afraid of Uriah Heep. I was angry and turned to Heep who had just walked into the room.

"What are you up to, Heep? I always thought you were a snake and now I see that I was right! You're taking advantage of a good man like Mr Wickfield."

"Does a good man drink and not take care of his business records? If I wasn't here, this 'good man' you speak of would be out in the streets!"

"Oh, and I suppose you saved him, did you?"

"Yes, and I'm going to save Miss Agnes, too. I'm … I'm going to marry her!"

The blood pounded in my head and for some reason, I was unable to speak. I wanted to kill Uriah Heep in that instant, and I decided to do all that I could to prevent this marriage.

In the meantime, there were other problems to deal with. Aunt Betsey had lost most of her money through Mr Wickfield's bad business decisions. I was sure that this had something to do with Uriah Heep. My aunt and Mr Dick came to live with me in London, and I helped them as much as I could.

I was also very worried about my wife. Dora was very ill. My aunt looked after her in the day while I was at work. In the evenings I would rush to her bedside and gently stroke her soft hair, and whisper to her that I loved her. On one dark, stormy evening not long after her illness began, she asked to see Agnes – alone.   45

While they talked, I sat downstairs by the fire and thought about all the happy moments my dear Dora and I had shared and how it hurt me to see her so ill and unable to move. When Agnes came back downstairs, I realised from the look in her eyes that my darling wife Dora had passed away.

Found - and Lost!

I fell into a deep depression after Dora's death. I decided that I would leave for Europe as soon as I had helped Agnes deal with the business concerning Uriah Heep and her poor father.

The only good news I had in those difficult and gloomy days was about Emily. It was extremely good news for Mr Peggotty, too. At last, he had found out where Emily was and what had happened to her.

She had travelled for months with Steerforth on the *Little Emily*. But Steerforth soon lost interest in Emily and she missed her family very much. They argued, and Steerforth told Emily that their affair was over. She returned to London alone, but felt too ashamed to ask her family to take her back.

Luckily, Mr Peggotty had never stopped looking for her. After months of searching through Europe, he found her in London. He told her to hush when she asked for forgiveness, and took her gently into his arms.

"I've always loved you, Emily and I always will. Now come, my dear child, and we'll start a new life, far away from here."

Mr Peggotty had taken rooms in London and decided to stay there with Emily while he prepared for them both to leave for Australia. I hoped that everything would turn out well for them.

In the meantime, Mr Micawber continued to act mysteriously. He came to my room one night when my aunt was there.

"Oh, I'm pleased to find you both here. I am too upset and angry to speak now and I'm not ready, but I ask you to meet me in Canterbury in one week. It's very important!"

Mr Micawber would not even stay for some of his favourite punch. He left quickly and was not at all like himself.

"I just don't understand it. Mr Micawber usually likes to stay and talk to me. Something is very wrong."

"It must have something to do with Heep, David," said my aunt.

"Yes, I never trusted that man."

I decided to visit Ham and Peggotty in Yarmouth before going to Canterbury to meet with Mr Micawber as he had requested. I was hoping to see the old Yarmouth that I remembered. When I arrived, the weather was very rough because a great storm had begun. I saw Ham on the beach, just as he was tying a rope around himself. He was going to swim out to sea, where a boat was sinking.

"Please, Ham! Don't go! It's too dangerous!"

"There's a boat in trouble out there, and people are going to die if I don't help."

Unfortunately, there was nothing I could do to stop him. I watched helplessly as the furious waves became higher and rougher. I thought I recognised the boat that Ham was trying to save. Suddenly, there was a bright flash of lightning, then a crash of thunder. A huge wave covered everything, and Ham and the boat disappeared under the water. I helped to pull the rope back in, but Ham was dead when we took him from the water.

The next morning a few pieces from the boat came ashore. I then knew why the boat out at sea had looked so familiar. One piece of wood that was washed onto the beach had the words *Little Emily* written on it! Ham had died trying to save Steerforth, the man who had taken Emily away from him. I decided not to tell Mr Peggotty or Emily what had happened.

How It All Worked Out

The deaths of Ham and Steerforth had made me very sad. They also reminded me again of my own dear wife's death. I tried to cheer myself up, and thought that it was now time for me to go abroad for a while. Before I did anything, though, there was a meeting I had to attend. I had to go to Canterbury to hear what Mr Micawber wanted to say.

My aunt was already there. So were Mr Wickfield, Agnes and Mr Micawber. Agnes looked more beautiful than ever. My smile soon faded when I remembered that she would get married to Heep soon. Mr Micawber was standing in front of us all with his glasses on, and he was holding a long sheet of paper. He was no longer acting mysteriously. He seemed confident, and looked like he had something very important to say.

"What I have here, my good friends, will make us all happy again, and will show us that good always wins over evil in the end! As you know, I work for a – a Mr Uriah Heep. You may have suspected that he could not be trusted. And you would have been right! Here is a list of all the papers he signed without Mr Wickfield's permission. I also have proof that he stole money, and that he used Mr Wickfield's name to steal the money of certain people, like Miss Betsey Trotwood here. But, like all criminals, he will lose – thanks to me!"

We all rose from our seats, and clapped and cheered with joy. Mr Wickfield and Agnes hugged. I was so glad that everything had turned out well that I had to express my appreciation to Mr Micawber.

"Mr Micawber, your behaviour confused me. It had crossed my mind that perhaps you were no longer the good man I once knew. I apologise for having thought badly of you. I want to thank you with all my heart for the good that you have done."

"Dear David, I had my doubts about Heep from the start, but I needed proof before I could say anything. That may explain why my behaviour might have seemed mysterious."

Things worked out rather well for everyone after that. The Micawbers paid their debts and then emigrated to Australia with Mr Peggotty and Emily. Mr Wickfield made sure that Uriah Heep went to prison.

Aunt Betsey returned to her cottage in Dover with Mr Dick, who wanted to get back to working on his book. Things were now better for Mr Wickfield, too, and Agnes would not have to marry Uriah Heep.

I soon left England as I had planned, and went to Europe. I took Agnes' advice and did something useful there. I decided to write again and to send my work home to be published. People bought my books and liked them. Soon, I became a well-known author.

A year later, I returned to England. First, I visited Aunt Betsey. She was overjoyed to see me. We talked far into the night and she told me all the news about my friends. But I was more interested in one person than anyone else.

"Aunt Betsey, have you heard any news from Agnes?"

My aunt smiled and looked at me strangely.

"She is more beautiful than ever. I think she may be in love … and perhaps she will marry soon."

I suddenly felt empty, as if I had lost something very precious.

"Do … do you know who the lucky man is?"

"It is not my place to say, David. These are just my suspicions."

"Then, if it's true, I'm sure Agnes will tell me when she sees me."

I should have felt happy for Agnes because she deserved to find true love, but instead I felt empty. The thought of her being

in love with someone else almost broke my heart. It was then that I realised that my feelings for her were far deeper than the love of a brother for a sister.

I arranged to visit Agnes at her home as soon as possible after that conversation. I found her alone, reading by the fire. When she saw me come in, she put her book down and welcomed me. We sat in one of the old-fashioned window-seats and talked. She looked very happy to see me.

"You shall become so famous soon, David, that it will be impossible for us to talk like this in the future."

"Then we must talk now – while I still can."

"You look very thoughtful today, David."

"My dear Agnes, do you doubt my being true to you?"

"No!" she answered, with a look of astonishment.

"You have a secret. Let me share it, Agnes."

She looked down and started to tremble. I continued.

"It is so strange to hear from someone else's lips that you are in love. If you can trust me as you say you can, let me be your friend, your brother. Do not shut me out of your happiness!"

She rose from the window and hurried across the room, as if she did not know where she was going, and burst into tears. I do not know why, but seeing her reaction filled my heart with hope. I went after her and took her arm, then looked into her beautiful blue eyes.

"Agnes! Sister! Dearest! What have I done! I cannot bear to see you like this. My dearest girl, dearer to me than anything in life, if you are unhappy, let me share the unhappiness. If you need help, let me give it to you. For whom do I live now, Agnes, if not for you?"

"Don't speak to me now, David … don't! I'm not myself. Another time …"

That was all I could distinguish through her tears.

"I must say more. If you think that I cannot be happy for you and let you marry a good man of your own choice, you are wrong and I don't deserve it!"

"That's not true. Whenever I needed help or guidance you have given it to me. If I have any secret, it is not a new one. And I cannot reveal it. It has been mine for a long time and must remain mine."

She tried to leave again, but I stopped her.

"Agnes, stay! A moment!"

Her words were going through my mind, giving me new hope.

"Dearest Agnes! Whom I respect and honour so – whom I love with all my heart! When I came here today, I thought that nothing would have made me say this. I wanted to keep it secret until we were old. But if I have any hope to ever call you something more than Sister …"

New tears started rolling quickly down her face. She looked at me, and my heart leapt. They were tears of joy!

"Agnes! Forever my guide, my best support! You were always so much better than me. And I needed you to be there for me always – to listen to my every hope and dream … so I did not realise that my first and greatest love was for you. I went away, loving you; I stayed away, loving you; and I returned home, loving you. I know that now – and I will never let you go!"

"You are the only person I have ever loved, David! I did not tell you this before, because I was afraid that you did not feel the same way about me."

"Oh, Agnes! I would be the happiest man in the world if you married me!"

"I will marry you, David!"

On the day of our wedding, while we were celebrating with our friends and family, she turned to me and whispered,

"My dearest husband, there is one thing I must tell you."

"Let me hear it, my love."

"It is about the night when … Dora died."

"Yes?"

"She wanted to ask me a favour … a last request."

"And it was …?"

"That only **I** would take her place."

My beautiful Agnes put her head on my chest and cried; and I cried with her, even though we were so happy.

My story is almost finished. Agnes and I married and I am now a happy family man with three children and a successful writing career. One day, as we sat together by the fire, an unexpected visitor arrived. It was Mr Peggotty! He had done well in Australia and had come back to thank me for everything, but especially for not telling him and Emily about Ham's death before they left. If they had known about it earlier, they would probably never have gone, and their lives would not have been so successful. He also told me that Mr Micawber had become a governor! So his honesty finally paid off and he had become respected and popular in his new country.

When I look back, I see that I had good times and bad times, but I suppose 'that's life', as the saying goes. I'm certain of one thing though – kindness conquers all. I am grateful for the good people I met and for the way my life finally turned out.

Activities

Beginnings

Read or listen to Chapter 1 and write *T (True)* or *F (False)*.

1 David's father died before David was born. ....
2 Aunt Betsey became David's godmother. ....
3 Aunt Betsey was pleased when David was born. ....
4 David did not like Mr Murdstone. ....
5 Peggotty had a brother in Blunderstone. ....

What do you think?

A Discuss the following questions.

1 Why do you think David's mother needed Peggotty so much?
2 What do you look for in a friend?
3 Did you know anyone that you did not like when you first met them, but changed your mind once you knew them better? What made you change your mind about this person?

B Find the following extracts from Chapter 1 and discuss their meanings.

1 p. 8: "... *Aunt Betsey marched into our house and gave everybody her opinions from the beginning.*"
2 p. 8: "*I* (David's mother) *will not have you talk about my late husband in this manner!*"
3 p. 10: "... *Peggotty was much more than a servant.*"

Language Practice

I Look at the words and pictures to make phrases from Chapter 1. Then choose one phrase and draw a picture of it. The class must guess which one you have drawn.

1 late .... 4 .... of gold.

2 fall .... 5 expect a ....

3 rock a .... 6 fold your ....

II Fill in the gaps with the correct form of the word in capitals.

1 The Queen has a .... to take care of her clothes.   **SERVE**
2 There was another .... on the roads because of people driving too fast.   **DIE**
3 I got up late and, ..., missed my bus to school.   **FORTUNE**
4 How can I .... that I didn't steal the pen?   **PROOF**

What happens next?

Look at the three ideas below and guess which one happens next. Choose one and write notes to continue the story in your notebook.

Mr Murdstone does something to hurt David.	David stays in Yarmouth and doesn't go back home.	David discovers that Mr Murdstone is a good person after all.

My First Trip and Homecoming

 Comprehension

Read or listen to Chapter 2 and answer the questions.

1 What did David think about Yarmouth when he first arrived there?
2 Who did David meet in Yarmouth?
3 What was strange about the Peggottys' house?
4 What did Emily want to do for Mr Peggotty?
5 How was David's home different when he got back from Yarmouth?
6 What happened when David could not answer the question?
7 What did David do to Mr Murdstone?
8 How was David punished again?

What do you think?

A Discuss the following questions.

1 Why do you think David's mother married Mr Murdstone?
2 How are the holidays you usually take different from the one David had in Yarmouth?
3 How do you think a child should be punished if he/she has not done his/her homework?

B Find the following extracts from Chapter 2 and discuss their meanings.

1 p. 14: "... I (Emily) *don't suppose I'm from the right sort of family ...*"
2 p. 16: "*It just didn't feel like home anymore.*"
3 p. 16: "*Mr Murdstone had not only changed the atmosphere of The Rookery, but he had also changed Mother.*"

Language Practice

I   Fill in the gaps to make collocations from Chapter 2.

pipe	school	secret	fishy	watch	room

1   e.g. ......*secret*......... wish   4   boarding ....
2   silver   5   .... smell
3   living   6   gold ....

II   Fill in the gaps with the correct form of the verbs in the box.

cost	hold	beat	bite	throw

1   The dog .... the boy on his leg.
2   When David was naughty, Mr Murdstone .... him.
3   "That dress looks very expensive. How much did it .... ?"
4   The children .... the ball at the window and broke it.
5   It was a wonderful feeling when I .... my daughter
    for the first time.

Guess the meaning

*Read the following paragraph and guess the meanings of the
words/phrases that are printed in bold.*

It was the first day of winter exams and I didn't
want to go to school. When the alarm clock went
off, **I dragged myself out of bed** and got ready. I
packed my pens and books, then walked to school.
There were lots of children at the school gates,
shouting. They seemed to be excited and **looking
forward to** their exams! At nine o'clock, we all went
inside. Then the **headmaster** met us and gave us some
amazing news! He told us that the weather had been very cold
and **frosty** and the heating was not working. So he sent the teachers
home. No more **schoolwork** for the rest of the week. Hurrah!

School Days

Read or listen to Chapter 3 and circle the correct answer.

1 David saw .... Bridge when he first arrived in the city.
  a Tower   b Salem   c London

2 Mr Creakle was the .... at Salem House.
  a headmaster   b teacher   c boy

3 When David first went home, his mother had a new ....
  a husband   b baby   c servant

4 David was glad to go back to school because he liked the
  ....
  a headmaster   b food   c schoolwork

5 One day Mr Creakle gave David the most terrible ....
  a news   b beating   c schoolwork

6 When David went back home the second time, he was a/n
  ....
  a half-brother b man   c orphan

What do you think?

A Discuss the following questions.

1 Why do you think Mr Creakle did not beat Steerforth?
2 What are the advantages and disadvantages of boarding schools?
3 Do you have a favourite storybook? Talk about it with your partner.

B Find the following extracts from Chapter 3 and discuss their meanings.

1 p. 20: *"He (Creakle) walked up and down and stared at us with a look of disgust on his face."*
2 p. 22: *"Miss Murdstone told me (David) never to compare her brother's baby to me and said that the baby and I were not alike in any way."*

Language Practice

I Find the opposites and draw a line to join them.

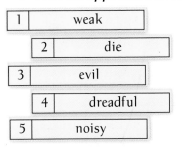

1	weak
2	die
3	evil
4	dreadful
5	noisy

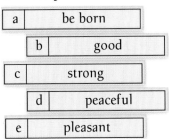

a	be born
b	good
c	strong
d	peaceful
e	pleasant

II Fill in the crossword.

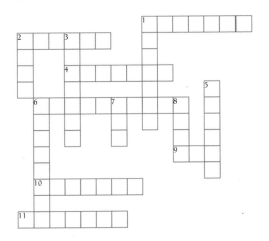

Across

1 You have five of these on each hand.

2 You can cross a river over a ....

4 Another word for surprised.

6 The area outside a church.

9 To touch something gently.

10 A feeling of not liking sb.

11 If you are in a place, you are ....

Down

1 When someone is dead, we go to their ....

2 The meat from a cow.

3 A feeling of strong dislike.

5 Very cold.

6 To think about.

7 To hold someone close.

8 Slightly wet.

67

Off to Work I Go

 Comprehension

Read or listen to Chapter 4 and put the following events in the correct chronological order.

a David goes to work at the wine factory. ....

b David goes to stay in Yarmouth. ....

c Mr Micawber goes to prison. ....

d Peggotty marries Barkis.   *e.g.* .....*1*......

e David decides to look for Aunt Betsey. ....

f Mr Micawber decides to leave London. ....

What do you think?

A Discuss the following questions.

1 Why was Yarmouth not as exciting to David as it was before?

2 Do you think that children should be allowed to or made to work? Why/Why not?

3 Should people go to prison if they cannot pay their debts?

B Find the following extracts from Chapter 4 and discuss their meanings.

1 p. 24: *"You will have to learn to make your own way in the world ..."* (Mr Murdstone to David)

2 p. 25: *"Annual income, twenty pounds; annual expenses, nineteen pounds; result - happiness! Annual income, twenty pounds; annual expenses, twenty-one pounds; result - misery!"*

3 p. 25: *"... I'm* (Mr Micawber) *stuck here in misery."*

Language Practice

1 Join the two halves to make complete sentences.

1	It is my first day at my new job, so it's off to …	a	… make your own way in the world.
2	If you have any spare money, you should …	b	… work I go.
3	They are very selfish and always …	c	… make me feel at home.
4	When you grow up, you must …	d	… want everything to themselves.
5	Whenever I go to my friends' houses, they always …	e	… save for a rainy day.

1 .... 2 .... 3 .... 4 .... 5 ....

II Match the phrasal verbs below to their meanings and pictures. Then draw the three missing pictures.

1 put aside   a to save (usually money)   i Draw the picture in your notebook

2 turn to sb   b to remember   ii

3 fall down   c to think of and tell people about a story/song etc.   iii Draw the picture in your notebook

4 make sth up   d go to sb for help   iv

5 think back   e to drop down onto the ground   v Draw the picture in your notebook

With My Aunt

Comprehension

Read or listen to Chapter 5 and complete these sentences using <u>one or two</u> words.

1 David knew that his Aunt Betsey lived about .... miles from London, in a place called Dover.

2 A young man with a donkey and .... stole all David's possessions.

3 David felt embarrassed when he reached Aunt Betsey's house, because he looked like a ....

4 Aunt Betsey put David on the sofa with a .... under his head.

5 Aunt Betsey said that the Murdstones were ....

6 David thought that Aunt Betsey was very .... and clapped his hands in delight.

What do you think?

A Discuss the following questions.

1 What kind of person do you think Aunt Betsey was?

2 Why do you think the Murdstones went to Aunt Betsey's house?

3 When Aunt Betsey took David in she said, *"All I ask is that you respect us and follow our simple rules."* What do you think these rules were?

B Find the following extracts from Chapter 5 and discuss their meanings.

1 p. 29: *"I (David) took a deep breath when I saw a tall woman (Aunt Betsey) with a straight back walk out of the house."*

2 p. 30: *"I (David) watched her (Aunt Betsey) with my heart in my mouth as she marched back into her garden."*

3 p. 32: *"... she (Betsey) slammed the door behind them."*

Language Practice

What was the conversation like when the Murdstones came to visit Aunt Betsey? Here are some suggestions. You may use your own ideas if you prefer.

Yes, of course. You know all about discipline, don't you?

You know, we always did our best for David.

Then I don't know why I came!

I suppose David told you that!

I will take my chances with David.

I insist that you keep quiet!

Aunt Betsey:	Well, what are we going to do about David Copperfield?
Miss Murdstone:	He always was a wicked and lazy child.
Mr Murdstone:	Please, sister. Let me speak. Miss Trotwood, **(1)** ....
Aunt Betsey:	By sending him to work in that dreadful factory, you mean?
Mr Murdstone:	He needed to learn the discipline of work.
Aunt Betsey:	**(2)** ....
Miss Murdstone:	His mother did not discipline him at all!
Mr Murdstone:	**(3)** ....
Miss Murdstone:	**(4)** ....
Aunt Betsey:	Neither do I, but I know that you were both very cruel to David **and** his mother.
Miss Murdstone:	**(5)** ....
Aunt Betsey:	Yes, and I believe him.
Mr Murdstone:	David is an evil boy and you will find that out for yourself, Miss Trotwood!
Aunt Betsey:	**(6)** ....
Mr Murdstone:	You are making a big mistake!
Aunt Betsey:	Now leave my house and I never want to see or hear from either of you again!

71

Life with the Wickfields

 Comprehension

Read or listen to Chapter 6 and answer the following questions.

Who ...
1 ... chased away the donkeys?
2 ... was writing a life story?
3 ... was the headmaster of the school in Canterbury?
4 ... did David live with in Canterbury?
5 ... was like a sister to David?
6 ... reminded David of a snake?
7 ... did Uriah Heep live with?
8 ... visited Uriah Heep's house while David was there?

What do you think?

A Discuss the following questions.

1 Why do you think Mr Dick's relatives really wanted to put him in a mental institution?
2 What do you think you will do in the future?
3 Should we judge people from their appearance or manner?

B Find the following excerpts from Chapter 6 and discuss their meanings.

1 p. 34: *"Living there* (in Aunt Betsey's) *was like something from a storybook."*
2 p. 34: *"No one knows the future. But you can prepare for it by doing well at school and learning from your mistakes."* (Agnes to David)
3 p. 36: *"... I* (Heep) *am the humblest person in the world."*

Language Practice

1 Scan Chapter 6 and find 12 adjectives that can be used to describe a person. Then, put them in the appropriate column. Some may be used more than once.

Appearance	Manner	Personality	Mood

II Read and circle the correct item.

1 It is important to save for the ....
   a father   b future   c present

2 The .... spoke to me because the manager was busy.
   a assistant   b woman   c business

3 When I went to prison, my .... helped get me out.
   a teacher   b lawyer   c assistant

4 There was a /an .... at the door and I opened it.
   a appearance   b subject   c knock

5 James had important .... to discuss with his boss.
   a business   b future   c subject

6 Sally was worried about her .... and was always buying new clothes.
   a father   b appearance   c present

7 Our .... sometimes tell us when something is dangerous, and they are usually right.
   a marks   b father   c instincts

Old and New Friends

Comprehension

Read or listen to Chapter 7 and then match the beginnings and endings of the sentences below to make true statements.

1 David's first real job was at   a) Yarmouth.
2 David met Steerforth at   b) a dinner party.
3 There was an engagement   c) the theatre.
   party in   d) Spenlow and Jorkins' law
4 Steerforth met Emily at   offices.
5 David fell in love with Dora at   e) an engagement party.

What do you think?

A Discuss the following questions.

1 Why do you think Steerforth called his boat the *"Little Emily"*?
2 If you had a boat, what would you call it? Tell your partner.

B Find the following extracts in Chapter 7 and discuss their meanings.

1 p. 38: *"I (David) reminded him (Steerforth) of a fresh daisy at sunrise."*
2 p. 39: *"You've turned out better than any niece I could have hoped for!"* (Aunt Betsey to David)
3 p. 40: *"Davy, I'm (Dora) a silly little thing. Perhaps you should have chosen someone clever like Agnes instead of me."*

Language Practice

1 *This is a summary of the story so far. Fill in the gaps with a word from the box and then put the paragraphs in the correct chronological order.*

law	kind-hearted	engagement	wine factory
strict	born	decides	handsome

A ☐   David goes to live with Mr Micawber, a **(1)**......... man. When Mr Micawber leaves London, David decides to run away to Aunt Betsey's. She looks after him well and he goes to a new school. He meets Uriah Heep and Agnes.

B ☐   Mr Murdstone is very **(2)** .... and cruel. One day, he asks David a difficult question which he cannot answer. He beats David and David bites Mr Murdstone's hand. Mr Murdstone **(3)** .... to send David away to school.

C ☐   David does well at school and joins the **(4)** .... offices of Spenlow and Jorkins. He meets Steerforth in London and invites him back to Yarmouth to visit the Peggottys where there is a/n **(5)** .... party. David meets Dora Spenlow, falls in love and they get married.

D ☐   David's father dies before David is **(6)** ...... and after a few years, his mother meets the **(7)** .... Mr Murdstone. Peggotty, their servant, takes David to Yarmouth and when David gets back, he finds that his mother has married Mr Murdstone.

E ☐   David goes to Salem House where he meets Steerforth. David's mother dies while he is at school. Mr Murdstone does not want David at The Rookery and sends him away to work in his **(8)** ....

What happens next?

Write T (True) or F (False) and discuss your answers with your teacher.

1 Agnes decides to live with David and Dora.   ....
2 Emily and Steerforth run away together.   ....
3 Ham and Emily get married and move to London.   ....
4 Emily leaves Yarmouth alone and moves to London. ....
5 David and Dora go to live abroad.   ....
6 David decides to leave Dora.   ....

An Unsettling Time

 Comprehension

Read or listen to Chapter 8 and tick (✓) the correct answer.

1 One day, David had a visitor: ☐ Mr Micawber.
☐ Mr Peggotty.

2 Emily had run away with ☐ Steerforth.
☐ Ham.

3 David received a letter from ☐ Agnes.
☐ Emily.

4 Mr Micawber was working for ☐ Mr Wickfield.
☐ Uriah Heep.

5 One of the people who had lost money was ☐ Aunt Betsey.
☐ Mr Dick.

What do you think?

A Discuss the following questions.

1 What kind of person was Uriah Heep?
2 How do family members help each other when they are in trouble?

B Find the following extracts in Chapter 8 and explain their meanings.

1 p. 43: *"... she's (Emily) a good girl ... She may have made mistakes ..."*
2 p. 45: *"... how can you (Micawber) work for a man like Heep?"*
3 p. 45: *"If I (Heep) wasn't here, this 'good man' you speak of would be out in the streets."*

1 *Find the following phrases in Chapter 8 and guess their meanings. Then choose one, draw a picture and ask your partner to guess which one it is.*

1 to expect the worst ....

2 to take advantage of sb ....

3 the blood pounded in my head ....

....

4 in the meantime ....

5 in that instant ....

II *After Emily disappeared from Yarmouth, Mr Peggotty was very worried. He put posters up all around the area to find her. Write out the poster for him. You need to include:*

• *her name*

• *her appearance (height/build/hair/eyes/etc)*

• *her age*

• *what she was wearing when she was last seen*

• *who and where to contact if she is found*

• *possible reward*

Use 60-80 words.

Found - and Lost!

 **Comprehension**

Read or listen to the following extracts from Chapter 9 and correct the mistakes.

1 I decided that I would leave for Europe as soon as I had helped Agnes deal with the business concerning Mr Micawber and her father.

2 They argued and Steerforth told Emily that their marriage was over.

3 Mr Peggotty had taken rooms in Canterbury and decided to stay there with Emily.

4 In the meantime, Mr Micawber continued to act normally.

5 There's a man in trouble out there, and people are going to die if I don't help.

6 A huge wave covered everything, and Ham and the boat appeared under the water.

1	................=......................	4	................=......................
2	................=......................	5	................=......................
3	................=......................	6	................=......................

What do you think?

A Discuss the following questions.

1 Was Mr Peggotty right to take Emily away from England?

2 Do you think people should 'run away' from problems?

3 What do you think Steerforth was doing in Yarmouth?

B Find the following extracts from Chapter 9 and discuss their meanings.

1 p. 47: "*I* (David) *fell into a deep depression after Dora's death.*"

2 p. 49: "*Unfortunately, there was nothing I* (David) *could do to stop him* (Ham)."

Language Practice

Use words from the box to complete the phrases. Then make up a story using the words from the box.

lose	search	turned	crash	huge	rough	washed

1 After the accident, everything .... out well in the end.
2 If you have lost your book, you must .... for it.
3 An old bottle was .... up onto the beach.
4 The .... weather made the ship sink.
5 I don't want to .... my way, so I'll ask a policeman.
6 A loud .... of thunder frightened Sally and she ran into her house.
7 There was a .... pile of letters waiting for me when I got back to work.

Guess the meaning

Read the following paragraph and guess the meaning of the words/phrases that are printed in bold.

Mark opened the envelope and **cheered with joy**. His wife came downstairs to see why he was so happy. The book he had written was going to be **published**! He had been writing it for many years but always **doubted** that anyone would be interested, but now someone was! Suddenly, **a thought crossed his mind**. He remembered that when they got married, they had planned to go and live **abroad** – maybe Australia – but because they had no money, it did not **work out**. After a few years, he became a **family man**, and his children were at school. But now, they were grown up and, if he became an author, he could work where he liked. His wife was **overjoyed** and smiled when she heard the news. One thing is **certain**. If you work hard, it **pays off** in the end.

How it all worked out

 Comprehension

Read or listen to Chapter 10 and match the actions to the people. One action may be used more than once.

Agnes ▢▢▢

Aunt Betsey ▢▢

David ▢▢▢

Mr Micawber ▢▢▢

Mr Peggotty ▢

Uriah Heep ▢

1 ... went to the meeting in Canterbury.
2 ... would probably marry Uriah Heep soon.
3 ... had been stealing money.
4 ... had been behaving very strangely.
5 ... went back to Dover.
6 ... would soon become famous.
7 ... was in love with David.
8 ... had three children.
9 ... came back from Australia.
10 ... became a governor in Australia.

What do you think?

A   Discuss the following questions.

1 Why do you think David and Agnes never told each other how they felt before?
2 Is it sometimes a good idea to keep your feelings and other things (e.g. bad news) to yourself?

B   Find the following extracts from Chapter 10 and discuss their meanings.

1 p. 53: *"I* (David) *suddenly felt empty, as if I had lost something very precious."*
2 p. 56: *"... do you* (Agnes) *doubt my* (David) *being true to you?"*

David went on holiday to Yarmouth. This is still a popular holiday destination for the British today. Seaside holidays have been popular since Victorian times, when people started to realise that the fresh sea air was healthy. This was especially important to people living in London, because it was a very dirty city in Victorian times. Everyone had coal fires in their homes and the smoke hung over the city causing very thick fog called a 'pea souper'. London's nickname in those days was 'The Smoke'. To begin with, only the rich had the time and money to take holidays at all, but now nearly everyone takes at least one holiday a year.

I   *What are the popular holiday destinations in your own country? Talk about them in class.*

II   *Do you think it is important to take time out for holidays? Why/Why not?*

What's the moral?

A moral is a lesson about what is right or wrong that you can learn from a story. What do you think the moral is in 'David Copperfield'? Choose from those listed below or make up your own.

- Life goes on, no matter what happens to you.
- Always look for the best in people; they will never let you down.
- Everybody has a good side if you look for it.
- Honesty and kindness pay off in the end.
- When things go wrong, try again.
- Blood is thicker than water.
- Love conquers all.
- Trust your instincts - they are usually correct.
- Always look on the bright side of life.

Your own ....

JOBS

1   A number of different jobs were mentioned in 'David Copperfield'.
    See if you can match the jobs to the characters from the story.
    Some may be used more than once.

II What other jobs can you think of? Write down as many as you can think of and then compare your list with that of your partner.

My list

....	....	....
....	....	....
....	....	....
....	....	....
....	....	....
....	....	....

III Put the jobs into different groups under the following headings and make posters. Jobs with People, Jobs with Machinery, Creative Jobs and Jobs with Animals. Some of the jobs will fit into more than one category.

Jobs with People	Jobs with Machinery	Creative Jobs	Jobs with Animals
....	....	....	....
....	....	....	....
....	....	....	....
....	....	....	....
....	....	....	....
....	....	....	....
....	....	....	....
....	....	....	....
....	....	....	....
....	....	....	....
....	....	....	....
....	....	....	....

IV Find a picture of someone doing one of the jobs you found or draw a picture of someone doing this job.

83

Change the Story!

Summaries do not need to be written in paragraphs. They can also be told through a flow diagram.

What if David's mother did not marry Mr Murdstone? Then the later action would change. The two alternatives are below.

This is what actually happened:

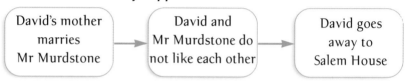

This is what could have happened:

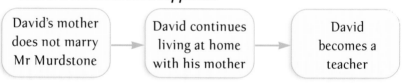

As you can see, the change in one action affects the rest of the story. The characters make decisions which affect later action.

a) *Make a list of the key events in the story. Think about the choices the characters had to make at each of these key events and make a list of these, too (e.g. David's mother marries Mr Murdstone, David bites Mr Murdstone, etc).*

b) *Think what would have happened if the characters had made different choices at each key event and make a list of the alternatives.*

c) *Choose one of these key events and re-write the story in flow diagram format, based on the alternative decision the character made.*

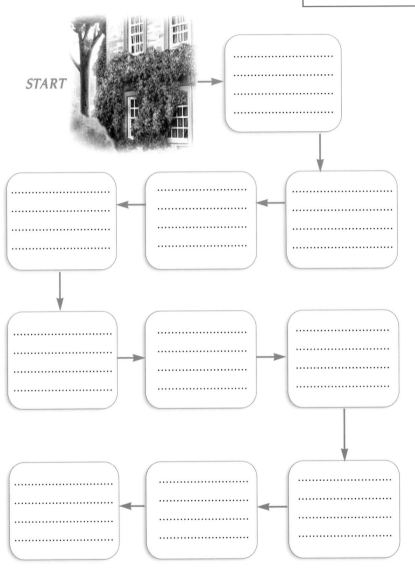

START

What is the new moral of your story? ....
....

Word List

Look these words/phrases up in the dictionary and fill in their meanings.

Chapter 1

a type of (phr) ....

admit (v) ....

although (conj) ....

attitude (towards sb/sth) (n) ....

be born (v) ....

be close by (phr) ....

be jealous (v) ....

bear sth (bore-born) (v) ....

beard (n) ....

beginning (n) ....

birth (n) ....

certainly (adv) ....

chat (v) ....

cheeks (n, pl) ....

curl (v) ....

death (n) ....

deceased (adj) ....

declare sth (v) ....

disappointed (adj) ....

dress up (phr v) ....

even though (phr-conj) ....

eventually (adv) ....

exactly (adv) ....

excited (adj) ....

expect a baby/child (phr) ....

fact (n) ....

fall asleep (phr) ....

feel safe (phr) ....

firm (adj) ....

firmly (adv) ....

fisherman (n, pl: fishermen) ....

fold one's arms (phr) ....

forehead (n) ....

giggle (v) ....

godmother (n) ....

grave (n) ....

handshake (n) ....

handsome (adj) ....

harsh (adj) ....

honest (adj) ....

immediately (adv) ....

in a huff (phr) ....

in this manner (phr) ....

juicy (adj) ....

laugh to myself (phr) ....

look (n) ....

look after sb (phr v) ....

luckily (adv) ....

male (n) ....

march (into a place) (v) ....

memories (n, pl) ....

miss sb/sth (v) ....

my late husband (phr) ....

nearby (adj) ....

nephew (n) ....

nest (n) ....

on this occasion (phr) ....

opinion (n) ....

outdoors (adv/n) ....

parlour (n) ....

particular (adj) ....

peaceful (adj) ....

peck at sth (v) ....

plump (adj) ....

property (n) ....

prove (v) ....

reason (n) ....

remain (v) ....

rock (a child) (v) ....

rook (n) ....

rookery (n) ....

separate (v) ....

servant (n) ....

shy (adj) ....

silly (adj) ....

slim (adj) ....

stare (at sb) (v) ....

take care (phr) ....

tender (adj) ....

therefore (adv) ....

think back (thought-thought) (phr v) ....

to get somewhere/anywhere in the world (exp) ....

to make the most of sth (exp) ....

treat (n) ....

treat sb badly (phr) ....

trust (v) ....

unfortunately (adv) ....

unkind (adj) ....

warmly (adv) ....

wicked (adj) ....

widow (n) ....

with a heart of gold (phr) ....

Chapter 2

allow (v) ....

another chance (phr) ....

atmosphere (n) ....

beach (n) ....

beat sb (beat-beaten) (v) ....

beg (v) ....

behave (v) ....

behaviour (n) ....

bite (bit-bitten) (v) ....

boarding school (n) ....

bright (adj) ....

button (n) ....

cane (n) ....

cheer up (phr v) ....

collect (v) ....

complain (v) ....

control oneself (v) ....

cost (cost-cost) (v) ....

daughter (n) ....

decide (v) ....

diamond (adj) ....

disappear (v) ....

discipline (n) ....

distant (adj) ....

divide (sth into) (v) ....

drag (v) ....

dreamy (adj) ....

dull (adj) ....

expect (v) ....

fear sb/sth (v) ....

fireplace (n) ....

fishy smell (phr) ....

frown at sb (v) ....

furniture (n) ....

gloomy (adj) ....

gold watch (phr) ....

harder (adv) ....

hold (held-held) (v) ....

homecoming (n) ....

I don't suppose (phr) ....

it did me no harm (exp) ....

it feels like home (exp) ....

jolly (adj) ....

keyhole (n) ....

lock (v) ....

lonely (adj) ....

love at first sight (phr) ....

lower one's head (phr) ....

make a wish come true (exp) ....

miserable (adj) ....

niece (n) ....

orphan (n) ....

part (v) ....

pay (paid-paid) (v) ....

permanently (adv) ....

plenty of time (phr) ....

promise (v) ....

proper (adj) ....

rarely (adv) ....

realise (v) ....

refuse (v) ....

relatives (n, pl) ....

sail (on the water) (v) ....

seaside (n) ....

secret wish (phr) ....

shell (n) ....

show sb kindness (exp) ....

silver pipe (phr) ....

sister-in-law (n) ....

speak in a whisper (exp) ....

sth comes to an end (exp) ....

strict (adj) ....

swish (v) ....

take sb aside (phr) ....

tear (n) ....

the right sort of family (phr) ....

third cousin (n) ....

though (adv) ....

throw (threw-thrown) (v) ....

trip (n) ....

turn into (phr v) ....

unpleasant (adj) ....

upstairs (adv) ....

velvet (adj) ....

waistcoat (n) ....

whisper (v) ....

whistle (v) ....

widowed (adj) ....

Chapter 3

affect (v) ....

a loud person (phr) ....

amazing (adj) ....

be alike (phr) ....

be scared of sb (phr) ....

beef (n) ....

boiled (adj) ....

brave (braver-bravest) (adj) ....

bridge (n) ....

bury (buried-buried) (v) ....

chimney (n) ....

choose (chose-chosen) (v) ....

churchyard (n) ....

compare (v) ....

consider (v) ....

cruel (adj) ....

damp (adj) ....

disgust (n) ....

dislike (n) ....

drag oneself out of bed (exp) ....

dreadful (adj) ....

evil (adj) ....

except (prep) ....

fall down (fell-fallen) (phr v) ....

find out (found-found) (phr v) ....

finger (n) ....

frosty (adj) ....

funeral (n) ....

half-brother (n) ....

headmaster (n) ....

hug (v) ....

lazy (adj) ....

lip (n) ....

look forward to doing sth (phr) ....

news (n, pl) ....

noisy (adj) ....

obvious (adj) ....

pack (v) ....

pass away (phr v) ....

pat (v) ....

present (adj) ....

proudly (adv) ....

return (v) ....

satisfactory (adj) ....

schoolwork (n) ....

shape (n) ....

shocked (adj) ....

shout at sb (v) ....

similar (adj) ....

stale (adj) ....

the bell rings (phr) ....

tiny (adj) ....

touch (v) ....

unwelcome (adj) ....

weak (adj) ....

Chapter 4

act (v) ....

advice (n) ....

afterwards (adv) ....

agree (v) ....

annual (adj) ....

arrange (v) ....

as the saying goes (phr) ....

bad language (phr) ....

based on (phr) ....

be stuck (phr) ....

bored (adj) ....

borrow (v) ....

cart driver (n) ....

childish (adj) ....

comfort (v) ....

debt (n) ....

education (n) ....

exciting (adj) ....

expenses (n, pl) ....

expensive (adj) ....

feed (fed-fed) (v) ....

feel at home (exp) ....

fight (fought-fought) (v) ....

for a rainy day (phr) ....

for a while (phr) ....

grown-up (n) ....

here and there (phr) ....

ignore (v) ....

income (n) ....

irresponsible (adj) ....

kind-hearted (adj) ....

knock (v) ....

label (n) ....

laugh at sb (v) ....

low (adj) ....

make one's way in the world (exp) ....

Word List

make sth up (phr v) ....

misery (n) ....

move (v) ....

odd job (phr) ....

off (to a place) I go (exp) ....

owe (v) ....

prison sentence (phr) ....

protect (v) ....

put aside (phr v) ....

rat (n) ....

rather (adv) ....

result (n) ....

rough (adj) ....

run away (phr v) ....

save (v) ....

shine (v) ....

smelly (adj) ....

sob (v) ....

stick (stuck-stuck) (v) ....

suggest (v) ....

surrounded by (phr) ....

swear (v) ....

turn to sb (phr v) ....

wage (n) ....

want sth to oneself (phr) ....

warehouse (n) ....

wine factory (n) ....

wise (adj) ....

Chapter 5

amazed (adj) ....

approach (v) ....

back (n) ....

beggar (n) ....

bleed (bled-bled) (v) ....

bossy (adj) ....

burst into tears (phr) ....

by coach (phr) ....

cart (n) ....

cheerful (adj) ....

coach station (n) ....

comfortable (adj) ....

cottage (n) ....

desperate (adj) ....

detail (n) ....

donkey (n) ....

downstairs (adv) ....

drive off (phr v) ....

embarrassed (adj) ....

expression (n) ....

eyes become wide (phr) ....

fall apart (fell-fallen) (phr v) ....

fee (n) ....

field (n) ....

fit (adj) ....

follow a rule (phr) ....

fresh-baked (adj) ....

gardening glove (n) ....

gardening tool (n) ....

go through (went-been) (phr v) ....

handkerchief (n) ....

horrified (adj) ....

in delight (phr) ....

including (prep) ....

incredible (adj) ....

keep off (kept-kept) (phr v) ....

lawn (n) ....

lead sb (led-led) (v) ....

neat (adj) ....

never to be seen again (exp) ....

overhear (overheard-overheard) (v) ....

path (n) ....

pocket (n) ....

possessions (n, pl) ....

purpose (n) ....

rattling (adj) ....

reach (v) ....

remind (v) ....

remove (v) ....

rent (v) ....

respect (v) ....

rob (v) ....

set out (set-set) (phr v) ....

shawl (n) ....

situation (n) ....

slam (v) ....

snatch (v) ....

sofa (n) ....

stick out (of sth) (phr) ....

stiff (stiffer-stiffest) (adj) ....

straight (adj) ....

strength (n) ....

suffer (v) ....

sweet-smelling (adj) ....

take a deep breath (exp) ....

think over (thought-thought) (phr v) ....

throw sb out (threw-thrown) (phr v) ....

to one's horror (phr) ....

torn (adj) ....

tramp (n) ....

tyrant (n) ....

unable (adj) ....

well-kept (adj) ....

with my heart in my mouth (exp) ....

worried (adj) ....

Chapter 6

appearance (n) ....

assistant (n) ....

be aware (phr) ....

bother (v) ....

business (n) ....

care about sb (v) ....

catch (caught-caught) (v) ....

chase sb/sth away (phr v) ....

clear (adj) ....

dare (v) ....

do well (phr) ....

encourage (v) ....

enrol (v) ....

for that matter (phr) ....

frightening (adj) ....

future (n) ....

gentle (adj) ....

greasy (adj) ....

grin (v) ....

humble (adj) ....

ink-stained (adj) ....

insist (v) ....

instincts (n, pl) ....

interesting (adj) ....

knock (n) ....

lawyer (n) ....

likewise (adv) ....

mad (adj) ....

mature (adj) ....

mysterious (adj) ....

odd (adj) ....

peacefully (adv) ....

place sb (v) ....

polite (adj) ....

prepare (v) ....

pretend (v) ....

psychiatric institution (n) ....

skinny (adj) ....

slyly (adv) ....

storybook (n) ....

subject (n) ....

top marks (phr) ....

trouble (v) ....

trusted (adj) ....

truthfully (adv) ....

turn up (phr v) ....

twist (v) ....

uncomfortable (adj) ....

uneasy (adj) ....

well-educated (adj) ....

wonder (v) ....

Chapter 7

a silly little thing (phr) ....

bachelor (n) ....

be a success (phr) ....

celebrate (v) ....

concentrate (v) ....

confident (adj) ....

cosy (adj) ....

curl (n) ....

daisy (n) ....

daydream (v) ....

delicate (adj) ....

desire (n) ....

discussion (n) ....

dressmaker (n) ....

engagement (n) ....

fall madly in love with (exp) ....

fellow (adj) ....

fresh (adj) ....

good-hearted (adj) ....

grand-looking (adj) ....

hard-working (adj) ....

hush (v) ....

innocent (adj) ....

it didn't mean much to me (exp) ....

law offices (n, pl) ....

nickname (n) ....

particularly (adv) ....

part-time (adv) ....

profession (n) ....

raise (v) ....

satisfied (adj) ....

shake hands (phr) ....

show sb around (phr v) ....

sigh (v) ....

social class (phr) ....

sunrise (n) ....

thick (adj) ....

toast (n) ....

training (n) ....

turn out (phr v) ....

writer (n) ....

Chapter 8

bedside (n) ....

business records (n, pl) ....

darling (adj) ....

deal with (phr) ....

decision (n) ....

discover (v) ....

expect the worst (exp) ....

hurt (v) ....

in that instant (phr) ....

in the meantime (phr) ....

peculiar (adj) ....

prevent (v) ....

probably (adv) ....

raise sb (v) ....

rush (v) ....

share (v) ....

steal (v) ....

stroke (v) ....

take advantage of (phr) ....

the blood pounded in my head (exp) ....

trick (v) ....

unsettling (adj) ....

upset (adj) ....

urgently (adv) ....

wife (n) ....

Chapter 9

affair (n) ....

argue (v) ....

ashore (adv) ....

be ashamed (phr) ....

be washed onto the beach (phr) ....

Word List

concerning (prep) ....

cover (v) ....

crash of thunder (phr) ....

dangerous (adj) ....

depression (n) ....

extremely (adv) ....

familiar (adj) ....

flash of lightning (phr) ....

forgiveness (n) ....

furious (adj) ....

helplessly (adv) ....

huge (adj) ....

lose interest (phr) ....

mysteriously (adv) ....

pleased (adj) ....

pull (v) ....

punch (n) ....

request (v) ....

rope (n) ....

rough (weather) (adj) ....

save (v) ....

search (v) ....

sink (v) ....

storm (n) ....

tie (v) ....

turn out well (phr) ....

wave (n) ....

Chapter 10

a sheet of paper (phr) ....

apologise (for having done sth) (v) ....

appreciation (n) ....

astonishment (n) ....

attend a meeting (phr) ....

author (n) ....

be true to sb (phr) ....

break sb's heart (phr) ....

career (n) ....

certain (adj) ....

cheer with joy (phr) ....

chest (n) ....

conquer (v) ....

criminal (n) ....

deserve (v) ....

distinguish (v) ....

doubt (n) ....

doubt (v) ....

emigrate (v) ....

especially (adv) ....

express (v) ....

fade (v) ....

family man (n) ....

famous (adj) ....

far into the night (phr) ....

favour (n) ....

feelings (n, pl) ....

fill (v) ....

from someone else's lips (phr) ....

go abroad (phr) ....

good always wins over evil (exp) ....

good/bad times (phr) ....

governor (n) ....

grateful (adj) ....

guidance (n) ....

guide (n) ....

honesty (n) ....

honour (v) ....

hope (n) ....

hurry (v) ....

I'm not myself (exp) ....

impossible (adj) ....

it is not my place to say (exp) ....

last request (phr) ....

my heart leapt (exp) ....

of one's own choice (phr) ....

old-fashioned (adj) ....

overjoyed (adj) ....

pay off (phr v) ....

permission (n) ....

popular (adj) ....

precious (adj) ....

proof (n) ....

publish (v) ....

reaction (n) ....

respected (adj) ....

reveal (v) ....

roll (v) ....

shut sb out (phr v) ....

sign (v) ....

sth crosses my mind (phr) ....

strangely (adv) ....

successful (adj) ....

support (n) ....

suspect (v) ....

suspicion (n) ....

take sb's place (phr) ....

thanks to (sb) (phr) ....

that's life (exp) ....

think badly of sb (phr) ....

thoughtful (adj) ....

tremble (v) ....

unexpected (adj) ....

useful (adj) ....

visitor (n) ....

wedding (n) ....

welcome (v) ....

well-known (adj) ....

window-seat (n) ....

work out (phr v) ....